MW00883882

Captain Blownaparte and the Little Dragon

by Helga Hopkins
Illustrated by David Benham

Published as an eBook in 2019
Paperback edition published in 2019

contact@blownaparte.com

Words and Illustrations Copyright © 2019 Helga Hopkins & Roger Hopkins
Captain Blownaparte is a Registered Trademark

The moral right of the author has been asserted

All Rights Reserved

No part of this publication may be reproduced, distributed or transmitted in
any form or by any means, or stored in a database or retrieval system, nor be
otherwise circulated in any form of binding or cover, without prior permission
in writing from the author.

The characters in this publication are entirely fictitious. Any resemblance to
real people alive or dead is purely coincidental.

ISBN: 9781689774055

Captain Blownaparte™
and the Little Dragon

by Helga Hopkins & David Benham

Captain Blownaparte and
the Little Dragon

Captain Blownaparte and Pirate Pedro were wandering past the Pirate Tavern when they noticed Captain Purplebeard and his crew sitting outside in the sun. Now we all know that Purplebeard is the nastiest pirate on the seven seas, so it was no surprise that he suddenly stuck his foot out and sent poor Captain Blownaparte flying across the floor!

As Captain Blownaparte skidded along, his hook hand accidentally hit an extremely large egg tucked under Purplebeard's table. Suddenly, a crack opened up in the egg and a big blue eye peered right out at Captain Blownaparte. Then the crack quickly closed up again.

Back on the ship, Captain Blownaparte told the crew the story of the giant egg. But Prosper, the ship's clever parrot, became extremely worried. 'That sounds like a dragon's egg, and Purplebeard must have stolen it!' said Prosper. 'He probably wants his own personal dragon to help him control all the pirates on the planet, and he'll know that when little dragons hatch, they think the first person they see is their mum or dad!'

'Hmm,' mused the Captain, 'I think the baby saw me first.' Then he told Prosper about his fall. This made Prosper laugh so much that he fell off his perch and kept on laughing and spluttering for quite some time. When he recovered he said, 'So the baby dragon will think our Captain is his dad! I'd love to be there when the little thing hatches and sees Purplebeard!'

Meanwhile, on Captain Purplebeard's ship, the Captain and his crew were all gathered around the egg. Suddenly, it opened with a big crack, and a little yellow dragon hopped out of the shell onto the deck. Captain Purplebeard tickled him under the chin and said, 'Come to your daddy.' But the little dragon looked at him angrily and spat out a flame that set the nasty Pirate's hat alight!

Grumpy old Gertie quickly said, 'This needs a woman's touch!' But the little dragon didn't like her either, nor any of the other pirates who tried to tickle him. As a result, it wasn't long before all the pirates were smoldering! 'I've had enough of this,' boomed Muscles, the ship's largest pirate, 'Let's throw this little monster overboard!' But Gertie had a better idea, 'We'll send the dragon over to Blownaparte, and with a bit of luck this fire breathing monster will set his ship alight!'

Later, Captain Blownaparte was really excited to get a parcel addressed to him, he absolutely loved getting presents. But the parcel burst into flames before he could open it, and the little dragon flapped over to Captain Blownaparte and gave him a huge cuddle. Everybody took a great liking to the little dragon and Captain Blownaparte named him 'Junior'.

Sproggie looked very worried, 'Junior looks soooo hungry! I bet Purplebeard didn't feed him anything.' Then, right on time, Swiss Sepp came up on deck carrying two very large buckets of sticky toffee. He was preparing some more toffee cannonballs, but when Junior saw the toffee, he rushed over and gobbled up the whole lot!

'Oh dear,' said Sproggie. 'It's not very healthy to be eating so much sugar.' Prosper calmed him down, 'It might be bad for little boys and girls, but dragons need plenty of sugar as they burn it up when they breathe out their fire'. The little dragon snuggled up in Captain Blownaparte's arms and started to snore gently. It was quite funny to see and a bit dangerous too - as little flames danced around his nostrils every time he breathed out!

The peace was shattered when Pirate Tidy, the ship's cleanest pirate, came sliding down the mast at high speed. He'd been dusting the crow's nest and had seen something shocking in the distance. 'There's a huge dragon flying towards us!' he panted, being completely out of breath. 'It must be Junior's mum!'

Prosper shuddered with dread. 'That's really bad news. Angry dragons usually breathe fire before they ask questions. Does anyone have an idea what to do?' Swiss Sepp had the answer. 'We put Junior up on a chair in the middle of the deck and cover the floor with sticky toffee. That'll stick the dragon's mum to the floor and Junior can then explain that we're all the good guys.'

They'd just finished covering the deck with sticky toffee when the huge dragon landed on the ship. While she was trying to lift her feet off the toffee, Junior told her all about his adventures with the bad and the good pirates. Then the dragon calmed down and quickly realised she was stuck to the world's most delicious toffee. She and Junior melted the toffee with their fire and polished it off in moments. Alfredo, who loves to eat was very impressed, 'Even I couldn't have eaten so much toffee!'

Suddenly mummy dragon noticed Captain Purplebeard's ship in the distance and took off at high speed. 'Pleeeease don't eat them!' Captain Blownaparte yelled after her! Purplebeard and his crew had seen what was happening, and took off in their lifeboat, rowing madly! In the meantime, the angry dragon swiftly set light to their ship.

When the dragon returned, she blew a flame along Captain Blownaparte's ship. 'Wow! She's painted a dragon sign on the side of our ship,' squawked Prosper. 'That means we're under her protection and no dragon would ever do us any harm, and we can visit Junior on Dragon Island any time we like!'

They had a great big feast to celebrate. Swiss Sepp was quite exhausted at having to prepare so much sticky toffee for Junior and his mum, but they simply couldn't get enough of it!

Then after much kissing and cuddling, Junior climbed on his mum's back and they flew back to Dragon Island. 'We'll all miss Junior,' spluttered the Captain with a big shiny tear in his eye, but we can always pop in and see him when we're sailing near Dragon Island.'

PEDRO

ROSIE

CAPTAIN
BLOWNAPARTE

PROSPER

SPROGGIE

SPIKE

TURNIP

PIRATE TIDY

ALFREDO

SWISS SEPP

Made in the USA
Columbia, SC
07 January 2021

30491791R00022